WATCHMAN NEE

NEW BELIEVER'S SERIES

PRAYER

11

Living Stream Ministry
Anaheim, California

© 1993 Living Stream Ministry

All rights reserved. No part of this work may be reproduced or transmitted in any form or by any means—graphic, electronic, or mechanical, including photocopying, recording, or information storage and retrieval systems—without written permission from the publisher.

First Edition, November 1997.

ISBN 1-57593-967-3

Published by

Living Stream Ministry
1853 W. Ball Road, Anaheim, CA 92804 U.S.A.
P. O. Box 2121, Anaheim, CA 92814 U.S.A.

Printed in the United States of America
97 98 99 00 01 02 / 9 8 7 6 5 4 3 2 1

PRAYER

Scripture Reading: John 16:24; James 4:2-3; Luke 11:9-10; Psa. 66:18; Mark 11:24; Luke 18:1-8

I. PRAYER BEING A BASIC CHRISTIAN RIGHT

Christians have a basic right while living on earth today, the right to receive answers to prayers. The moment a person is regenerated, God gives him the basic right to ask of Him and to be heard by Him. John 16 says that God answers when we ask in the name of the Lord so that our joy may be made full. If we pray without ceasing, we will live a Christian life that is full of joy on earth today.

If we unceasingly pray, yet God does not unceasingly answer our prayer, or if we have been a Christian for years and God hardly or never listens to our prayers, there must be something seriously wrong. If we have been a Christian for three to five years without receiving one answer to prayer, we are ineffectual Christians. We are not just a little ineffectual, but very ineffectual. We are children of God, yet our prayers are never answered! This should never be. Every Christian should experience God answering his prayers. Every Christian should have frequent experiences of prayers being answered. This is a basic experience. If God has not answered our prayers for a long time, it means that there is surely something wrong with us. There is no way to deceive ourselves in the matter of answers to prayer. If it is answered, it is answered. If it is not answered, it is not answered. If it is effectual, it is effectual. If it is ineffectual, it is ineffectual.

We would like to ask every Christian: Have you learned to pray? Has God answered your prayer? It is wrong for prayers to be left unanswered, because prayers are not just a speaking into the air. Prayers are meant to be answered. Unanswered prayers are vain prayers. Christians must learn to have answered prayers. Since you have believed in God, your prayers should be answered by God. Your prayers are useless if God does not answer them. You must pray until your prayers are answered. Prayer is not only for spiritual cultivation but even more for receiving answers from God.

Prayer is not that easy a lesson to learn. A person may be a Christian for thirty or even fifty years and yet not learn to pray well. On the one hand, prayer is not a simple thing. On the other hand, prayer is so easy that a person can pray as soon as he believes in the Lord. Prayer can be considered the most profound as well as the simplest subject. It is so profound that some still cannot pray well despite learning about it all their lives. Many children of God feel that they do not know how to pray even up to the time they die. However, prayer is so simple that the moment a person believes in the Lord, he can start praying and have his prayers answered. If you begin your Christian life in a good way, you will always receive answers to your prayers. If you do not have a good start, you may not have an answer to prayer for three or even five years. If you do not have a proper foundation, you will need much effort to correct it later. Therefore, once a person believes in the Lord, he must learn to receive answers from God for his prayers. We hope that every believer will pay attention to this matter.

II. CONDITIONS FOR PRAYERS BEING ANSWERED

In the Bible we can see many conditions for having prayers answered, but only a few of them are basic. We believe that if we meet these few conditions, our prayers will be answered. These few conditions are equally applicable to those who have prayed for many years. These are very basic conditions, and we should pay attention to them.

A. Asking

All prayers should be genuine petitions before God. After a brother was saved, he prayed every day. One day a sister asked him, "Has God ever listened to your prayer?" He was surprised. To him prayer was just prayer; why did anyone have to bother about whether or not they were answered? From that time on, whenever he prayed, he asked God to answer his prayer. He began to consider how many of his prayers were answered. He discovered that his prayers were quite vague and capricious. It did not matter whether God answered them, and it did not matter whether God ignored them. They were like prayers to God for the sun to rise the next day; the sun would rise whether or not he prayed. He had been a Christian for a year, yet none of his prayers were answered. All that time he had been just kneeling and muttering words. He could not pinpoint what he had asked for. This amounted to not having asked for anything at all.

The Lord says, "Knock and it shall be opened to you" (Matt. 7:7). If what you are knocking on is just the wall, the Lord will not open the wall to you. But if you indeed are knocking on the door, the Lord will surely open the door to you. If you ask to go in as well, the Lord will surely let you in. The Lord said, "Seek and you shall find" (v. 7). Suppose that there are many things here. Which one do you want? You must ask for at least one thing. You cannot say that anything will do. God wants to know what you specifically want and what you specifically are asking for. Only then can He give it to you. Hence, to ask means to demand something specific. We have to ask. This is what it means to seek and to knock. Suppose you want something from your father today. You have to ask for the specific thing you want. If you go to a pharmacy for medicine, you must say exactly what medicine you want. If you go to a market to purchase vegetables, you must say what vegetables you want. It is strange that people can come to the Lord without saying what they want. This is why the Lord says that we need to ask and ask specifically. The problem with us is that we do not ask. The hindrance is on our side. In our prayers we need to speak what we need and what we want. Do not pray an all-inclusive prayer in a frivolous way, caring little whether or not it is answered.

A new believer needs to learn to pray. He needs to pray with a specific goal in mind. "You do not have because you do not ask" (James 4:2). Many people go through the motion of prayer without asking for anything. It is useless to spend an hour or two hours or even eight or ten days before the Lord without asking for anything. You need to learn to ask for something; you need to knock, really knock hard, at a door. Once you clearly identify the entrance and seek to go in, knock hard at the door. When you seek something specific, you will not be satisfied with just anything; you want that particular thing. Do not be like some brothers and sisters who stand up in the meeting to pray for twenty minutes or half an hour without knowing what they want. It is strange that many people have long prayers that do not ask for anything.

You must learn to be specific with your prayer. You should know when God has answered your prayers and when He has not answered your prayers. If it makes no difference to you whether or not God answers your prayers, it will be hard for you to effectively pray to Him if you come across a difficulty in the future. Empty prayers will not be effectual in times of need. If prayers are empty when needs are specific, one cannot expect any solution for the problem. Only specific prayers can deal with specific problems.

B. Not Asking Evilly

We should ask, but there is a second condition to prayer; we should not ask evilly. "You ask and do not receive because you ask evilly" (James 4:3). We should ask God out of necessity. We should not ask mindlessly, unreasonably, or wildly. We should never ask carelessly or evilly for any unnecessary things according to our lust or our flesh. If we do, our prayers will be in vain. While God often gives us "superabundantly above all that we ask or think" (Eph. 3:20), asking evilly is a different matter.

Asking evilly means asking beyond one's capacity or real need. If you have a need, you can ask God. But you should only ask God to take care of your need. Asking beyond what you need is asking evilly. If you have a great need, it is not wrong to ask God to satisfy such a need. But if you do not have a great need, and you ask for it, you are asking evilly. You can only ask according to your capacity and need. You should never ask foolishly for this and that. Asking carelessly is to ask evilly, and such asking will not receive any answer from God. Asking evilly before God is like a four-year-old child asking his father for the moon in the sky. God is not pleased with evil asking. Every Christian should learn to confine his prayers within the proper scope. Do not open your mouth rashly and ask for more than you actually need.

C. Dealing with Sins

Some do not ask evilly, but God does not answer their prayers. This is because there is a basic barrier between them and God—sin. "If I regard iniquity in my heart, / The Lord will not hear" (Psa. 66:18). If a person has obvious and known sins in his heart, yet is unwilling to drop or part with them, the Lord will not answer his prayer. (Note the words *in my heart.*) The Lord cannot answer a person's prayer when there is such a great hindrance.

What does it mean to "regard iniquity in my heart"? It means to keep a sin in one's heart, being unwilling to part with it. Such a person knows something is a sin, yet he continues to cherish it. It is not only a weakness in conduct or appearance but also a craving in the heart. This is different from the person spoken of in Romans 7. Although the person in Romans 7 has failed, he hates what he is doing. The person here, however, regards iniquity in his heart. This means he keeps the iniquity to himself and is unwilling and reluctant to let go of it. The sin remains not only in his conduct but also in his heart. The Lord will not hear such a one when he prays. So long as there is one sin, it will hinder God from answering our prayer. We should not keep any favorite sin in our heart. We should acknowledge all sins as sins and should put them under the blood. The Lord can sympathize with our weakness, but the Lord will not allow us to regard iniquity in our hearts. Our prayers will not prevail if we have removed all the sins outwardly but still regard them in our heart and are unwilling and reluctant to part with them. The moment we begin our Christian life, we have to ask for the Lord's grace to keep us from falling and to sanctify us in our conduct. At the same time, we must thoroughly reject all sins in our heart. We should not retain or regard any sin in our heart. Our prayer will be useless if sin remains in our heart. The Lord will not listen to such a prayer.

Proverbs 28:13 says, "He that covereth his sins shall not prosper: / but whoso confesseth and forsaketh them shall have mercy." You must confess your sins. You must tell the Lord, "I have regarded a sin in my heart. I cannot give it up. I ask You to forgive me. I want to forsake this sin. Please deliver me from this sin. Do not let this sin remain in me. I do not want it. I want to reject it." If you confess to the Lord this way, the Lord will forgive; you will receive forgiveness. Then, your prayer will be heard. You must never be loose in this matter. You will not receive anything if you do not ask. You also will not receive anything if you ask evilly. Even if you do not ask evilly, the Lord will not answer your prayer as long as you keep back a favorite sin and regard it in your heart.

D. Believing

A condition on the positive side for having prayer answered is faith. Faith is indispensable. Without faith, prayer is ineffectual. The story in Mark 11 speaks loudly of the need for faith in prayer. The Lord Jesus said, "All things that you pray and ask, believe that you have received them, and you will have them" (v. 24). We must believe when we pray. If we believe that we have received what we are praying for, we will have them. We hope that as soon as a person has received the Lord, even a week after his conversion, he will know what faith is. The Lord said, "Believe that you have received them, and you will have them." He did not say, "Believe that you *will receive* them" but, "Believe that you *have received* them." We should believe that we have received what we asked for, and we will have them. The believing that the Lord speaks of here is followed by its predicate *you have received*. What is faith? Faith is believing that we have received what we have asked for.

Christians often make the mistake of separating *believe* from its predicate *you have received*. They place it before the expression *you will have them*. They pray to the Lord thinking that it is a matter of great faith to "believe...and you will have them." They pray to the Lord that the mountain be taken up and cast into the sea, and they believe that it will be so. They think that this kind of faith is great faith. However, this is to move *believe* away from *you have received* and to place it before *you will have them*. The Bible says that we should believe that we have received, not that we will receive. The two are definitely not the same. Not only do new believers need to learn this, but even those who have been believers for many years need to learn this.

What is faith? Faith is the assurance that God *has* answered our prayer. It is not the conviction that God *will* answer our prayer. Faith is when we kneel down to pray and say in an instant, "Thank God! He has answered my prayer. Thank God! This matter is settled." This is to believe that we have received. A person may kneel down and pray and may rise and say, "I believe that God will definitely hear my prayer." The expression *will definitely hear* is wrong. No matter how hard he tries to "believe" in this way, he will not see any result. Suppose you pray for a sick person and he says, "Thank God! I am healed." His temperature may still be high; there may be no change in his symptoms at all. But his problem is over because he is clear within himself that he is healed. However, if he says, "I believe the Lord will surely heal my sickness," he will probably need to try harder to "believe." The Lord Jesus said, "Believe that you have received them, and you will have them." He did not say that you will receive if you believe that you *will* receive. If you turn this around, it does not work. Brothers and sisters, have you seen the key? Genuine faith lies in the phrase *It is finished*. Genuine faith is thanking God for having already answered your prayers.

We need to say a few words more about faith. Consider the matter of healing. We can find some solid examples of faith in Mark's Gospel. There are three sentences in the Gospel of Mark which bear special significance to prayer. The first relates to the Lord's power, the second to the Lord's will, and the third to the Lord's act.

1. The Lord's Power—God Can

Let us look at Mark 9:21-23, which says, "And He questioned his father, How long has this been happening to him? And he said, From childhood. And it has often thrown him both into fire and into water to destroy him. But if You can do anything, have compassion on us and help us. And Jesus said to him, You say, If You can. All things are possible to him who believes." The father said to the Lord Jesus, "If You can do anything...help us." The Lord Jesus repeated his word and said, "If You can." The Lord's "if You can" is a quotation of the father's "if You can." The Lord Jesus was repeating what the father said. The father said, "If You can do anything...help us." The Lord Jesus said, "If You can. All things are possible to him who believes." It was not a question of "if You can," but a question of whether or not he could believe.

When man finds himself in difficulty, he is usually full of doubt; he cannot believe in the power of God. This is the first thing we need to deal with. It may seem at times that the power of the obstacle is greater than the power of God. The Lord Jesus rebuked the father for doubting the power of God. In the Bible we seldom find the Lord interrupting a person as He did in this case. It seems that the Lord was angry when He said, "If You can." The Lord rebuked the father when the father said, "If You can do anything, have compassion on us and help us." What the Lord meant was, "How can you say, 'If You can'? What is this? All things are possible to him who believes. This is not a matter of 'if I can,' but a matter of whether or not you believe. How dare you ask if I can!" When God's children pray, they should learn to lift up their eyes and say, "Lord! You can."

Mark 2 records the incident of the Lord healing a paralytic. The Lord said to the paralytic, "Child, your sins are forgiven" (v. 5). Some scribes reasoned in their hearts, saying, "Why is this man speaking this way? He is blaspheming! Who can forgive sins except One, God?" (v. 7). In their hearts they thought that only God could forgive sins and that Jesus could not. They regarded forgiveness of sins as a great thing. But the Lord said to them, "Why are you reasoning about these things in your hearts? Which is easier: to say to the paralytic, Your sins are forgiven, or to say, Rise and take up your mat and walk?" (vv. 8-9). The Lord was showing them that to man it was a question of whether or not one could do it, but to God it was a question of which was easier. For man, it is impossible for anyone to forgive sins or to ask the paralytic to stand up and walk. However, the Lord showed them that He could forgive sins as well as make the paralytic rise up and walk. Both forgiving and making the paralytic rise up and walk were easy for the Lord. The Lord was showing them that "God can." In our prayer we need to know that "God can" and that nothing is too difficult for the Lord.

2. The Lord's Will—God is Willing

It is true that God can do everything, but how do I know that He is willing to heal me? I do not know His will. Perhaps the Lord is not willing to heal me. What should I do? Let us look at another story. Mark 1:41 says, "And He was moved with compassion, and stretching out His hand, He touched him and said to him, I am willing; be cleansed!" Whether or not God can do something is not the question here; rather, it is a question of whether or not God is willing. No matter how great His power is, what does it matter if He is unwilling to heal? If God does not want to heal us, the greatness of His power will be of no consequence to us. The first question that has to be settled is whether or not God *can,* but the second question that also has to be settled is whether or not God *will.* The Lord said to the leper, "I am willing." The Old Testament tells us that leprosy is a very filthy disease (Lev. 13—14). Whoever contacted a leper was defiled. However, the Lord's love was so great that He said, "I am willing." The Lord Jesus stretched out His hand and touched and cleansed the leper! The leper entreated the Lord, and the Lord was willing to cleanse him. Can it be that the Lord will not heal our illness? Can it be that the Lord will not answer our prayers? We can all say, "God can" and "God is willing."

3. The Lord's Act—God Has Done

It is not enough for us to know that God can and God will. We need to know one more thing—God has done. We need to go back to Mark 11:24, which we quoted earlier: "All things that you pray and ask, believe that you have received them, and you will have them." This tells us that God has done something already.

What is faith? Faith is not just believing that God can and will do something but also believing that God has done something already. God has accomplished it. If you believe that you have received it, you will have it. If you believe and are confident that God can and will do a certain thing because He has given you a word concerning it, you should thank Him, saying, "God has done it!" Many people's prayers are not answered because they are not clear about this point; they still hope that they *will* receive something. However, to hope means to expect something in the future, whereas to believe means to consider something as being done. Genuine faith says, "Thank God, He has healed me! Thank God, I have received it! Thank God, I am cleansed! Thank God, I have recovered!" When faith is perfect, it will not only say "God can" and "God wills," but also "God has done."

God has listened to our prayers! God has accomplished everything! If we believe that we have received it, we will receive it. Very often, our faith is a faith that believes in what we will receive. As a result, we never receive anything. We should have the faith that we have already received. Faith is always a matter of "having been done" rather than of "will be done."

Consider a simple illustration. A person has just heard the gospel. If you ask him, "Have you believed in the Lord Jesus?", he may answer, "I have." You may then ask, "Are you saved?" If he says, "I will be saved," you know that he is not saved. Suppose you ask him again, "Do you really believe that you *are* saved?" If he says, "I will surely be saved," you know that he is still not saved. You may want to ask him again, "Are you really sure that you *will be* saved?" If he answers, "I *think* I will," his words do not sound like someone who is saved. If one says, "I will be saved," "I will surely be saved," or "I think I will surely be saved," there is no guarantee that he is saved. If the person says, "I am saved," he has the right tone. Once a man believes, he is saved. Any faith, if it is faith at all, believes in what has been accomplished. For example, once a person possesses faith at the time of his salvation, he immediately says, "Thank God, I have received." Let us lay hold of these three things—God can, God wills, and God has done.

Faith is not a psychological exercise. *Faith is receiving God's word* and believing with much assurance that God can, God wills, and God has done. If you have not received His word, *do not take the spiritual risk of trying to tempt God.* The exercise of psychology is not faith. Take illness as an example: All who are healed through genuine faith are not afraid of a medical checkup (Mark 1:44). The result of a medical checkup for those who have experienced a genuine divine healing will prove that it was a genuine healing rather than something psychological.

When new believers learn to pray, they should pray in two stages. In the first stage they should pray until they receive a promise. They should pray until they receive God's word. All prayers begin by asking God for something. Such prayers can continue for a period of time, sometimes lasting for three to five years. One needs to keep asking. Some prayers are answered quickly, while other prayers continue to go unanswered for years. This is the period of time when one needs to continue to ask. The second stage begins from the time one receives a promise and extends to the time the promise is realized. It begins from the time one receives God's word and extends to the time His word is fulfilled. This stage is not for praying, but for praising. In the first stage one prays, but in the second stage one praises. In the first stage he prays until he receives a word. In the second stage he praises the Lord continuously until the word is fulfilled. This is the secret to prayer.

Some people only know two points about prayer: First, they pray on their knees for what they do not have, and second, they have it; God has given it to them. Suppose I ask for a watch from the Lord, and after a few days the Lord gives me a watch. There are only two events: being without something and having something. Some do not realize that there is another event in between these two—the event of faith. Suppose I pray for a watch and one day say, "Thank God, He has already heard my prayer." Although my hands are still empty, I am clear within that I already have the watch. Indeed, after a few days the watch arrives. We cannot be concerned with just two events: not having and then having. We must be concerned with a third event—an additional event between not having and having, in which God gives us a promise, and then we believe and rejoice over it. Perhaps we have to wait three days before we actually receive the watch. But in our spirit, we received it three days ago already. A Christian should experience this kind of *receiving in the spirit*. If a person never experiences this kind of receiving in the spirit, he does not have faith.

We hope that new believers will know what faith is, and we hope that they will learn to pray. Perhaps, you have prayed continually for three or five days, a month, or even a year, and still your hands are empty. But deep in your heart, you have a little assurance that the matter will eventually be accomplished. At that time you should begin to praise God. You should continue praising Him until you have received the thing in your hand. Simply put, the first stage is to pray from nothing to having faith, and the second stage is to praise from having faith to actually receiving.

Why should we divide our prayers into these two stages? Suppose a person prays from having nothing to having faith. If he continues to pray, he may lose his faith. Once a person has acquired faith, he should begin praising. If he continues to pray, he may pray away his faith and not receive anything in the end. "You will have it" is an actual having in the hands, while "you have received it" is a having in the spirit. If the faith is already there, but the things have not materialized, one has to remind God with praise; he should not try to remind Him with prayer. If God has said that He will give us something, what else do we need to say? If we have the inward assurance that "we have received it," what more do we need to pray for? Many Christians have the experience that as soon as their prayer strikes faith, they can no longer continue to pray. They can only say, "Lord! I praise You." They have to keep their faith and praise, "Lord! I praise You. You have heard my prayer. I praise You because You answered my prayer a month ago." If you do this, you will receive. Unfortunately, some people do not have the knowledge. God has already promised them something, yet they still pray. In the end their prayer drives away their faith. This is a great loss.

The word in Mark 11:24 is too precious. In the whole New Testament, we cannot find another passage that explains faith as clearly as this one. "All things that you pray and ask, believe that you have received them, and you will have them." If a person sees this, he will know what prayer really is, and prayer will be a powerful tool in his hands.

E. Persevering in Asking

Another point about prayer which requires attention is that we must persevere in prayer and never stop praying. Luke 18:1 says, "They ought always to pray and not lose heart." Some prayers require perseverance. One has to pray to such an extent that the prayer seems to wear out the Lord and force Him to answer. This is another kind of faith. The Lord said, "Nevertheless, when the Son of Man comes, will He find faith on the earth?" (v. 8). This faith is different from the faith spoken of earlier, but they are not contradictory. Mark 11 says that we must pray until we have faith. Luke 18 says that we must ask again and again. We must have the faith to pray to the Lord persistently until one day He is compelled to answer our prayer. We should not care whether or not there is a promise. We should just pray until God is compelled to answer.

Many prayers are inconsistent prayers. A person can pray for one or two days. But after three months, he completely forgets it. Some people can pray about something only once. They cannot even pray a second time for it. Such ones care little whether they receive what they ask for. Please count how many of your prayers have been offered for the second time, the third time, the fifth time, or the tenth time. If you have forgotten your prayers, how can you expect God to remember them? If you do not have a heart to pray, how can you expect God to have a heart to listen? If you have forgotten your prayer, how can you expect God to remember it? Actually, you have never wanted what you asked for. A person will pray persistently only if he has a real need. One prays persistently only when he is pressed in the environment and driven by needs. In such cases he may persist for decades and still not give up praying, "Lord! If You do not answer me, I will not stop asking."

If you want to ask for something, you should trouble God about it. If you really want it, you must ask persistently until God hears you. You have to ask in such a way that God cannot do anything except answer your prayer. You have to ask until God is forced to answer you.

III. THE PRACTICE OF PRAYER

Every Christian should have a prayer-book, one a year. He should record his prayers as one keeps books in accounting. Each page should be divided into four columns. The first column should record the date he begins to pray for something. The second column should record the prayer item. The third column should record the date the prayer is answered, and the fourth column should record how God answers the prayer. In this way, one will find out how many things he asks God for in a year, how many prayers God answers, and what prayers are still unanswered. New believers should definitely keep such a book. But it is good for those who have been believers for many years to keep a prayer-book also.

The advantage of writing things down in a prayer-book is that it shows us whether or not God is answering our prayers. Once God's answers stop, something must be wrong. It is good for Christians to be zealous in serving the Lord, but such service is useless if their prayers are not answered. If a man's way to God is blocked, his way to men is also blocked. If a man has no power before God, he will have no power before men. We must first seek to be a man of power before God before we can be useful before men.

A brother once wrote down the names of one hundred forty persons and prayed for their salvation. Some names were recorded in the morning and the persons were saved in the afternoon. After eighteen months, only two on the list remained unsaved. This is a very good pattern for us. May God gain more Christians who will keep a record of their prayers. I hope you will put this into practice. Write down the items you are praying for one by one and the items that God has answered. Any item that has been recorded in the book, but has not received an answer, should be followed up by persistent prayer. You should only stop if God shows you that a certain prayer is not according to His will. If He has not shown you this, pray persistently until you receive an answer. You should not be careless in any way. You should be strictly trained in this matter from the beginning. You should be this serious before God. Once you pray, do not stop until you receive an answer.

In using the prayer-book, note that some items require daily prayer while others require prayer only once a week. The schedule depends on the number of prayer items you have in your prayer book. If you have little to ask, you can pray daily over every item in the book. If there are many items, you can arrange for certain items to be prayed over on Mondays and others to be prayed over on Tuesdays. Just as men schedule their time to do other things, we should set aside a specific time every day for prayer. If our prayers are not specific, we will not need a prayer-book. If our prayers are specific, we will need a prayer-book. We can place this book in the same place we put our Bible and hymn book. They are to be used daily. After a period of time, count how many prayers have been answered and how many prayers have gone unanswered. It is a blessing to pray in a specific way according to a prayer-book.

As for the prayer that the Lord teaches us in Matthew 6, the prayer of 1 Timothy 2, and prayers for light, life, grace, and gifts for the church, these are general subjects for prayer. They should not be classified under ordinary items for prayer. We should pray for these great things every day.

Prayer has two ends—the person who is praying and the one who is being prayed for. Many times, the one being prayed for will not change unless the praying one is first changed. If the situation on their side remains unchanged, we need to seek after God concerning our side. We should say, "O Lord! What changes do I have to make? What sins have I not dealt with yet? What loves should I forsake? Am I really learning the lesson of faith? Is there anything else I should learn?" If there is a need for change on our side, we must change first. We cannot expect those who are being prayed for to change while there is no change at all on our side.

Once a person believes in the Lord, he must learn to pray earnestly. He must learn the lesson of prayer well before he can have a deeper knowledge of God and a fruitful future for himself.